I0521259

# Storylandia

## The Wapshott Journal
## of Fiction

Issue 25

The Wapshott Press

Storylandia, Issue 25, The Wapshott Journal of Fiction, ISSN 1947-5349, ISBN 978-1-942007-17-3 is published at intervals by the Wapshott Press, now a 501(c)(3) nonprofit, PO Box 31513, Los Angeles, California, 90031-0513, telephone 323-201-7147. All correspondence can be sent to The Wapshott Press, PO Box 31513, LA CA 90031-0513. Visit our website at www.WapshottPress.org to learn more.

Storylandia is always seeking quality original short stories, novelettes, and novellas. Please have a look at our submission guidelines at www.Storylandia.WapshottPress.org or email the editor at editor@wapshottpress.org

Cover: "Green Grass, Castle" by https://bit.ly/2GIojRl

# Storylandia

## The Wapshott Journal of Fiction

Founded in 2009

Issue 25, Spring 2018

Edited by Ginger Mayerson

## Miranda

By Kelly Ann Jacobson

# Miranda

By Kelly Ann Jacobson

# ROSEMARY

Miranda saw Rosemary for the first time across her father's Poconos estate. It was summer; the garden overflowed with tomatoes, beans, and squash that sat like children hiding in the stalks. The flowers, sunflowers like bonnets and purple gladioli, stood with their faces to the sun; and the pool, a glacial blue body, sunned in the dazzling yellow light. The woman was small in the distance, childlike as she bent to pick something from the stretch of green life next to her, and Miranda only identified her as a woman when she bowed at the waist to reveal curves Miranda had just acquired a few years before.

"At least tell me she's older than me." Miranda turned to look at her father, who stood next to her with hands in his seersucker suit pockets admiring the view of his natural empire, and he squinted at her from below his hat and then grinned.

"She's older than you."

Miranda put her hands on her hips. "By a number in the single digits?"

"Why don't you meet her first and then judge her, Peanut?"

"Don't call me that."

"Very well then, Miranda, go say hello."

She put her duffel bag down on the thick pad of grass with a satisfying *whump*, probably the jostle of hair appliances, and then took a step towards the stranger on her way to becoming the third Mrs. Anderson. Rosemary's hair was as light red as an orange

Gerbera Daisy, a detail Miranda had not expected in the girlfriend of a man who dated former models with blond hair and anorexia, and it shimmered against the starchy white of her sundress. Rosemary, unaware of the incoming assault, bent down and grasped a green bean between two fingers, pulled the pod free, and popped it in her mouth with a crunch audible from over ten feet away.

"I think you're supposed to wash those first," Miranda said as she came within talking distance.

Surprised, Rosemary put a hand over her mouth and blushed. As she finished chewing, the two young women looked at each other, and Miranda was glad she had chosen to wear a tight purple dress and black sandals that tied up her taut ankles to her knees.

"I grew up on a farm," Rosemary said. "I used to run out into the fields and eat as many vegetables as I could get my little hands on, at least until my father would find me with skins and rinds scattered around me and would put me in time out."

*Don't smile, don't make a joke, don't become her friend.*

"I feel like I know all about you from your father, he talks about you all the time."

Miranda forced a laugh. "Funny, I heard about you from the driver who picked me up at the airport because my father was 'otherwise engaged.' From that sparkle on your finger, which I recognize as my mother's former wedding ring, I now realize he meant both figuratively and literally."

"I'm sorry, I didn't realize–"

"No, you wouldn't have. You're both too busy drinking expensive red wines and bobbing around the pool to think about how any of this could affect me."

"Miranda–"

"My best guess? My father woke up this morning as my plane landed, drank his orange juice while reading the Washington Post, took a horse ride to 'survey the kingdom' as he likes to say, and then watched golf. Nowhere in that busy schedule was the pause where most people would have asked, 'Hey, I wonder how my daughter will react to a woman practically her age becoming her new stepmother? Maybe I should have mentioned that small detail before I threatened to pull her college tuition to force her to spend the summer with me in the middle of nowhere without friends or the one parent who actually considers her feelings.'"

"Just let me–"

"Oh, and I'll go a bit further and speculate that he doesn't really care about me visiting at all. I'm here to train you: to polish those rough edges, get you ready for prime time at Rolling Hills Club, teach you how to style your hair and do charity projects in heels and a dress that packs you in like a sausage."

Silence. That one had hit home, and Miranda went in for the kill.

"He likes you because you're different, but deep down, my father is a politician who needs a politician's wife. In less than a month, you'll transform into one of us, identical and dispensable, and soon he'll drop you for a newer model like he dropped my mother and the wife who went before her. Take this ride for all it's worth, Rosemary, because it won't last long." Miranda turned away and walked towards the house; she had done what she came here for, and yet that night, she couldn't forget the tears in Rosemary's eyes as she left her in the garden, alone.

~~~

The next morning, Rosemary and Ray were already halfway through breakfast by the time Miranda emerged through the terrace doors. Her father read the newspaper, hiding all but the gray hair on top of his head, and Rosemary stared at an Alice Hoffman novel in front of her plate. The cook had prepared garden omelets with tomatoes and peppers from the garden served with freshly squeezed orange juice that he strained twice because her father hated pulp, but when the portly man tried to set a plate in front of her, Miranda waved him away.

"I'm not hungry, Juan, but thank you. Can you just bring me a cup of coffee with cream and two sugars?"

Juan's chin dropped, but he removed the omelet quickly and backed towards the kitchen. "Yes, Miss Anderson, right away."

Once the cook was out of earshot, Miranda's father looked up from his newspaper and gazed at her over his black-rimmed glasses. "You're going to hurt the old man's feelings."

"He doesn't want to be here anymore than I do," Miranda shot back. "How much did you have to pay him to leave his family for the summer?"

"Juan wanted to be here," her father replied, gazing back at his newspaper and killing the conversation.

"Speaking of travel," Rosemary chimed in, "I was wondering if I might take Miranda on a little trip today?"

"I don't think that's–" Miranda started to say, but her father cut in.

"What a wonderful idea! You two need some bonding time, and I could use a day off on the golf course."

"A day off from what, retirement?" Miranda muttered under her breath as Juan came back in with her coffee, set the white china cup and saucer down, and winked at her.

"Perfect, then it's settled," Rosemary said as she took Ray's wrinkled hand in her smooth one. "We'll be back by dinner; you'll barely miss us."

"I'm sure." Miranda scraped her chair back from the table, lifted her cup, and carried it to the door.

"Miranda?" Rosemary asked.

She paused without turning around.

"Can we meet at the car in an hour?"

"Fine. What should I wear?"

"Something comfortable."

They drove for about half an hour in Rosemary's silver Land Rover, a gift from Ray but certainly not his taste. Miranda had decided it was a Banana Republic day, white cotton pants and a strapless white top, coupled with a pair of Coach flats and movie star Aviators. Rosemary wore jeans, probably bought with her own money since Miranda didn't recognize the brand, a white peasant top, and a floppy straw hat that hid her eyes as they bumped over godforsaken dirt roads. *Abbey Road* hummed from the speakers— Miranda's favorite Beatles album as well, though she did not mention it, and right as "I Want You" finished its ominous three-minute repetition of a guitar riff, Rosemary stopped the car, turned off the engine, and listened.

"We're here," she said, though they were in the middle of a dirt road in the middle of abandoned farmland where there were no signs, mailboxes, or people to mark the "here" where they apparently were.

Rosemary hopped out of the car but left the keys in the ignition, so Miranda plucked them out before following her to a field of dried summer squash plants and pumpkin vines.

"I told you I grew up on a farm, but what I didn't tell you was that my mother never fed me from her garden." Rosemary found the hint of a trail in the middle of the field and began walking towards a house in the distance, so Miranda followed, trying not to think of her $500 shoes and the way the dirt already clung to them like fungus.

"We were so poor that every piece counted, and we children were the closest thing to farm hands my parents were ever going to get. Every once in a while I'd catch my mother popping a juicy red strawberry in her gap-toothed mouth when she thought I wasn't looking, but I had to wait until dinner to eat whatever leftovers we had from the day's sales."

The stray vines crunched beneath their feet like shattered egg shells, and as the house loomed closer, she could hear the call of Eastern Towhees—"Drink your tea" they chastised, a call her mother used to imitate while training Miranda for her afternoons at the Club.

"I never had dolls growing up," Rosemary continued, "I guess she thought they would make me crave the beautiful things I could never have. But her way was worse; it made me long for those beautiful things, dream about them as I fell asleep, and draw them in my notebooks. When I got my first job at your father's law firm, I bought the most beautiful doll I could find: a princess in a pink tulle ball gown. She stands on my dresser, a constant reminder of where I came from."

The house stood in front of them, a charred

wreck of wood and stone, and the wind rolled over the hills and through the house like a whistle.

Rosemary bent to pick up a splinter of black bark. "She never left the farm, just let it die around her like a flower plucked from its stem. Eventually, she left a lamp burning too long, and it set the whole place on fire. It took them a week to locate my brother and me because no one in town had seen us in over ten years."

Finally, she turned to face Miranda and held out the bark. Miranda took the chunk of rough wood in her hand and studied it; the ridges were gray like the strata of a rock formation.

"You were right about what you said yesterday. I love your father, he's the only family I have, but I know his character well. I won't end up back on this farm if he dumps me for a younger model, as you so adeptly put it... I think I'd rather die than come back." Rosemary faced the wind, and her red hair blew like flames across her face.

Miranda thought for a while as she stared at the house, its walls caved inward like a sinkhole, and then she took off her sunglasses. For the first time, she carefully switched off the malice in her voice. "Did my father tell you why he bought the Poconos estate?"

Rosemary shook her head. "The Poconos was how we started talking in the first place; he mentioned loving the forests and farms up here in a meeting one time, but he never really explained it."

"How like him. He didn't buy this house... well, he paid for it, but my mother picked it out. She was born here, on a farm just like you, and she loves the birds and the forests and the rivers more than anything in the world. During their divorce, he wouldn't let her have it, he dangled it like a carrot and then yanked it away, and she ended up in the city house amidst the roar of traffic she hated."

"So you'll help me?"

"It seems I must."

"Thank you, Miranda."

Rosemary hugged Miranda, and as she squeezed, the younger girl could not remember the last time her mother or father had touched her. Long gone were the days of nannies who cuddled and played with her, the sweet Mrs. Benson who tucked Miranda in at night and kissed her on the top of her head. She let herself enjoy the warmth for a few seconds, the duet of their two heartbeats, and then forced herself to step back.

"One more thing," Miranda added, looking Rosemary directly in the eyes. "A warning: leave this farm behind, but don't ever forget it. Desperation will be your best motivation, and trust me, you'll need it."

ADELITA

The large sitting room of the Rolling Hills Club was empty, save for the flickering candles and the menus that stood like protecting arms around their flames. The tables were covered with empty wine glasses, cocktail glasses, and snifters floating on napkins or abandoned on the side tables. Stray napkin balls sat like cats under the sofas and littered the floor. Unbeknownst to one of the guests asleep in her bed, a strand of pearls lay between the plush red sofa cushions. The cleaning woman will come into the room at five-thirty in the morning, find it, and hand it to the General Manager for safekeeping until the owner can be found. When no one comes to claim them—*after all, what are a few pearls to these women?*—one of the receptionists will grow bold and stick the strand in her pocket.

Jared, the current receptionist on duty since eleven, was witness to the last hours of the private bash. He watched the women float out on the arms of their husbands, their expensive furs like comforters around their shoulders and matching hats already perched to protect them from the cold. Most of them did not say goodbye to the old man as they left, but Jared was used to being part of the wallpaper. In fact, he preferred it that way; he could blend in, and from a quiet corner observe the activities of the privileged few who spent their nights drinking expensive alcohol and conversing with friends and enemies alike.

One of the last guests to leave the party was a woman in a striking black dress with small black sequins in triangular patterns across her chest and down her curvy thighs. As she approached the coat check to get her fur, a thick black coat that the attendant had already grabbed in anticipation of the beautiful woman's departure, she caught sight of another member of the Club down the hall and called out to her,

"Louisa!" she said to the other woman, waving a pale white hand in the air towards her. Both Jared and the attendant turned to look, and Jared was surprised to see that the beautiful woman's acquaintance was an older woman who lacked all of the young woman's style and social savvy. She was dressed in sensible black pants and a matching black blazer, with a white button-up shirt underneath that matched the streaks in her hair. No makeup adorned her face, but she did wear an expensive broach on the lapel of her blazer that had the profile of a young woman imprinted in gold. It could have been her face from younger years, or just a family heirloom; either way, it sparkled in the light of the chandelier above her head. Jared recognized her as the woman staying in Room #618, their largest suite.

"Hello Miranda, it's been too long," the older woman said, approaching the younger woman and putting out her hand.

"Too long, indeed—it's been over ten years! Tell me that you're giving up your romantic notions about owning a farm and are moving back to the city!"

The older woman smiled, but it was only a half-smile. "I'm sorry to disappoint you, but I'm just in town for the weekend."

"Business or pleasure?" Miranda asked as a cocktail-induced giggle escaped her lips.

"Death."

The giggles stopped, but Miranda struggled to keep her smile in check. Every few seconds the expression rippled over her face and then disappeared, like waves washing over sand.

"I am so sorry for your loss," she finally said. "May I ask whom?"

"My husband," Louisa said, looking up towards heaven, though to Jared it looked like she was inspecting the light fixtures instead.

"Oh, I had no idea..."

"No one did," the older woman said. "It's been a long time since we were last in town."

The grandfather clock in the hallway chimed twelve, and the younger woman was startled. "Oh, I really must be going. Harold will be waiting for me as drunk as a lord!" Miranda kissed Louisa once on each cheek, grabbed her fur with the swoosh of a matador tempting a bull, and disappeared.

Louisa turned to Jared for the first time since she arrived with her suitcase and brand new BMW, but though she looked him in the eye, she did not speak. Then she turned on her heels and disappeared into the elevator, leaving only the smell of peppermint candy behind.

Adelita approached the back door of the Club like she would a doctor's office, hugging her thin coat to her chest against the cold Philadelphia wind and taking a deep breath when she reached the stairs. At five in the morning, few other workers were on the street, but she had a lot to do before breakfast opened at seven. One cook was in the kitchen prepping for that day's events, and a fellow housekeeper talked on the phone in Chinese while Adelita put on her uniform. She had always thought it was strange that housekeeper uniforms still included skirts and aprons that made bending and kneeling impossible. Plus, they were useless as a screen door against the heavy air conditioning in the guest bedrooms. The younger members skipped stockings in favor of bare legs, but the housekeepers dutifully covered their skin with nylon.

Twenty years had gone by since Adelita had first applied for a job at the Club, and for that number, she had worn the same uniform, cleaned the same rooms, and washed the same chefs' clothes. The linens had been replaced many times, but the three daytime housekeepers remained to press and smooth them over the small twin beds in the guest bedrooms upstairs.

After she grabbed her cart full of cleaning supplies, trash bags, and a broom, Adelita rode the elevator up three floors to the guest bedrooms assigned to her when she originally got the job. Each housekeeper was in charge of a floor, except alternating coat check personnel and extra projects for Club events, and Adelita loved her floor the best because it was the only one composed entirely of guest bedrooms. As she cleaned, she imagined that the ornate decorations were her choosing and the beds were those of her children and sisters, and that the large suite at the end of the hall was where she and her husband resided. Unlike her fellow housekeepers, on the sixth floor, she was rarely interrupted by managers ten years her junior or guests arriving at the Club to play bridge or tennis. She worked in peace, letting the silver candlesticks and gold mirrors transport her to an alternate reality where she was the queen of a well-kept castle.

Then she heard a noise from #618 and froze. It sounded like a sniffle, the kind of noise her children made when a cold was coming, but it was heavier and louder than someone just blowing his or her nose. She approached the door slowly, her black work shoes made for soft treading, and the noise grew louder; it sounded like a woman was crying inside. Before Adelita could determine how many others were in the room, one of the floorboards creaked beneath her feet, and someone approached the door directly in front of her, listening to her as she listened back.

The door swung open to reveal an older woman in her mid-sixties dressed to go out in the cold winter weather. She wore a black wool coat down to her knees, a black dress that peeked through the slit of the open coat, black wool gloves, and a matching hat that sat like a small bowl on her head. Her makeup was flawless despite her watery eyes, and her only jewelry was a pair of pearl earrings.

"Can I help you?" the woman asked, her chin tilting up like proud royalty as she looked at Adelita.

"No ma'am," Adelita said, casting her eyes down on the rug. "I thought the room was supposed to be empty."

"I see." Their eyes remained on parallel planes for a few seconds, and then the woman put her chin down and let out a sniffle. "You're right, I was supposed to be at the church an hour ago. The service starts in thirty minutes, and I'm going to miss it because I can't pull myself together."

Adelita knew she should turn around and go back to work, but curiosity prompted her to ask, "What service?"

"A funeral, for my husband. We moved to the country ages ago, but we have many friends in this area who will want to pay their respects."

Adelita had lost her own husband more than five years ago in a car accident, and she remembered how she clung to her sister's arm for the entire ceremony; Rosa had red nail marks on her arm for a week, but she never made Adelita let go.

"Can't one of those friends come get you? It's easier that way."

"*Friends* is a loose term. Business associates is closer. And no, I would never ask them to come get me... they are probably too busy primping to bother with a silly old woman like me."

Adelita didn't know what primping meant, but she did know that she was lucky to have friends and family who had stuck with her through the burial and who took care of her daughter while grief incapacitated her. She looked at her cart—the mop and broom waiting like soldiers, the trash bags like tongues hanging from their brown boxes—and thought about all the work she had to do. Then she thought about those nail marks on enflamed flesh, the transfer of her grief to someone who could take it, and she put a hand out to Louisa.

"I'll go with you."

The old woman took her arm without hesitation. Adelita felt the weight on her arm, the transfer of pain through her veins, and she remembered standing in front of Mario's casket, watching him sink to the depths of earth waiting to swallow him whole, listening to the sound of her children crying behind her. To do it alone... unthinkable.

"Wait," the woman said, and then she disappeared into her room. Adelita heard rustling, and then the woman returned with a silky black dress that tied like a robe. "You can have this. It should fit; it ties around your waist."

"Oh, I couldn't–"

"You must, unless you have a fancy black dress hiding in your locker. Keep it... I have hundreds."

The fabric was as soft against Adelita's skin as the wedding dress she kept in the back of her closet; it was the last really nice dress she had worn, the last time silk touched her work-roughed skin.

"Thank you," she told the old woman, but Louisa waved her away.

Miles from the club, there were hundreds of dresses hanging in her closets, as lifeless as bodies in the ground. The farm was silent; even the animals paid their respects by saving their bleating and banter for the next sunrise. The halls were empty, the beds cold, the land untended. The groundsman took the day off to lie with his wife in their house on the edge of the land, mourning the loss of a kind boss more than any of those at the funeral home that day mourned a lost acquaintance. And in the city when Louisa dug her nails into Adelita's arm, she did not pull away.

THE BALL

"Lida, remember that you're in charge of Abby while we're gone." Her mother struggled to bend on one knee in her tight black dress, the one covered in black sequins that looked like their guinea pig's shiny eyes, and took Lida by the shoulders. "Make sure she gets a snack before bed at nine, and don't let her watch too much TV."

The smell of Adriana's perfume, a mixture of lavender and vanilla that came in a gemlike purple glass, suffocated Lida like a comforter on a warm night. She pulled away from her mother's grasp before the scent set off an allergy attack.

"I know, mom!" Lida said with a roll of her eyes. "You've only told me this every weekend since I was ten. That's–" she paused to calculate "–208 times."

"When did you get so smart?" her dad asked from the coat closet where he was searching for his black dress coat.

"I've always been this smart. You just didn't notice," Lida whispered under her breath.

"Aha!" her father said, holding the coat like a freshly hunted pelt as he stumbled from the closet. He shoved each of his large arms into the sleeves, then tried to button the front over his rotund belly. "Maybe I should have tried it on before November. It seems a bit snug."

"It's all those lecture dinners we've been going to at Rolling Hills," Adriana said with a shake of her head. "It's not healthy to eat that many courses. That's why I always request a fruit plate dessert. If we have time, we can stop by Saks and pick you up a new coat on the way over."

"But I like this one," Lida heard her father pout as she walked out of the foyer; she was already invisible, and they hadn't even left yet.

"Well, that one fit you twenty pounds ago," her mother retorted. "Unless you plan on re-hiring the trainer."

Lida walked up the winding stairs to the second floor, where she found her sister, Abby, playing with her dollhouse. Well, not playing exactly, more like accessorizing. She had strewn the miniature furs, white gloves, and ball gowns across the floor like a tornado's trail, and the blonde doll in her stubby fingers wore at least six necklaces and three jackets to which Abby was trying to add a fourth.

"How many coats does one girl need?" Lida asked as she pulled aside the white gauze canopy and lay down on Abby's four post bed. "You can put that one on a different doll."

"I don't like any of the other dolls," Abby explained, gesturing to a pile of discarded bodies in the corner of the room. "They're ugly."

"Then what's so special about this one?"

"She looks like mom."

Lida was tempted to explain that their mother was a natural brunette who was chubby as a teen, but refrained. Let Abby find the photographs hidden in the back of their mother's closet—a room even bigger than Abby's which housed rows upon rows of shoes, dresses, and business suits she wore to the country club—on her own. There had been a time when Lida snuck into Adriana's bathroom and tried on her red lipstick, sprayed her hairspray like perfume, and smeared eyeshadow on her cheeks because she wanted so badly to be as beautiful as her flawless mother, but that time was over, had ended with the photo of a happy teenage Adriana in loose bellbottom jeans and a lacy purple shirt back when her face could still express emotions. That was the girl Lida wanted to be.

A door slammed downstairs, and the two girls looked at each other in silence. The weight of their parents' departure hung over them like a heavy curtain, and for a minute neither of them moved.

"It's just you and me, squirt," Lida finally said. Then, in a cartoon voice that always made Abby giggle: "What'da you say to some TV and SpaghettiO's?"

When Mark and Adriana arrived at Rolling Hills Club, they found the entrance jammed with mostly BMWs and Ferraris, plus a few Priuses that belonged to the more liberal members of the club. There was a Rolls Royce angled over the grass on their left, from which a long, pale leg appeared and then the rest of Miranda Anderson followed. Adriana knew that no matter how many surgeries or bleaches or hours of training she completed, she would never look as flawless as her best friend, and she both loved and hated Miranda for it. Her hair was jet black, and she wore a stunning brown fur that made her look like a sexy spy in a James Bond movie.

"Adriana, darling!" Miranda squealed, abandoning her husband, Harold, to sort out parking with their driver. Harold was one of Mark's closest friends at the Club, though it always amused Adriana to see skinny, red-haired Harold next to Mark's generous frame as they drank Scotch on the Terrace or debated political strategies. "I don't know what has caused this breakdown in service, but we simply must go speak to the General Manager about it." Considering the General Manager was three rows in front of them parking cars while valets ran like chickens for seed, there didn't seem to be much of a point, and for a minute the two women watched the workers with a semblance of empathy.

"How about we go get ourselves a pre-cocktail cocktail instead?" Adriana suggested, taking Miranda's arm. Out of the corner of her eye, she looked Miranda up and down and was surprised to find that under her flapping fur coat, she wore a green dress shorter than that of a slutty high school girl at prom, and without any stockings no less. Her heels were over three inches, violating the understood shoe code and accentuating her bare legs even further, and the satin ties laced up her ankles like lingerie. Knowing her best friend, there was a purpose for her absurd attire, probably to 1) force gentlemen to flirt with her, then 2) make Harold uncontrollably jealous before the night was over so that 3) he would buy her a new car, purse, or whatever other item she had her eye on.

"I am in desperate need of refreshment," Miranda said as they entered the Great Hall. Adriana hesitated near the coat check, but Miranda walked right through the crowd to the young girl in a suit doing check-in for the Fall Ball and shoved her fur into the confused woman's arms.

"You can check this for me, can't you?"

"Sure, Mrs. Anderson," the woman said, but though her voice was sweet, Adriana could sense the undertone of anger that Miranda often caused in those who worked for her.

"Lovely, thank you. Oh, and... remind me of your name again?"

"Carrie."

"Right, Carrie. I was wondering if you could change my meal: something light, like a soup or salad, maybe a little plain chicken on top, and a fruit plate like Adriana always gets?"

"You mean for the meal served in half an hour?" Carrie asked, her face muscles tightening.

"Exactly."

Miranda signed her name on the receipt Carrie had put in front of her and walked away, leaving the girl in a panic and Adriana blushing as she found her own name and signed the chit without a word. As Adriana followed the sound of Miranda's high-pitched greetings in the bar, she heard Carrie run to the phone in the front office and call down to the kitchen, "I am so sorry, I know it's last minute, but you know how Mrs. Anderson is..." Yes, Adriana thought as she walked away, we do know.

The Fall Ball was exquisite: a four-piece jazz band played in the corner; the five-course meal satisfied even the most critical eye, and the dresses sparkled as the women shimmied and swung on the dance floor. There was a nice blend of old and new money in the room: old women with white hair and black lace dresses socialized with young girls in colorful gowns, and the gentlemen patted each other's backs and winked as their wives descended into reverie. Italian reds with hints of cherry and earth flowed with abundance as the servers discreetly refilled empty glasses and cleaned up those left on any available surface by nonchalant members, and the chocolate mousse served in a crystal dish looked like Abby's idea of heaven.

Abby. For a brief moment Adriana remembered her little girls at home alone, Lida only fourteen and already so old for her age, and the tiny pang of guilt she felt in her stomach surprised her. However, before she could ponder it further, she caught sight of Miranda's husband and observed his face turn a deep red and his eyes close to slits as he watched something in one of the other rooms. Then, without a word, he got up and walked away from their table.

Curious what Miranda had done now, Adriana pushed her chair back and stood slowly, testing her legs to see how drunk she was. The room spun, and the music seemed louder than before, trumpet blaring in her ear like a cat's yowl, but she was still confident she could make it across the room without stumbling. One step, then another, and with a few wobbles of her high heels she followed Harold up a flight of stairs and into the hotel portion of the club.

The whole floor was silent, and she crept as quietly as she could behind Harold's heavy footsteps. Suddenly, he turned to the right and entered one of the guest bedrooms, and Adriana peeked around the doorpost and watched as he flooded the room with light.

On the bed was Miranda, who rolled off her prey as soon as Harold flipped the switch. Mark, who lay splayed on the bed, had a harder time getting up, and he had to roll over and then push up with his arms to stand. He was obviously drunk, and when he tried to speak, his words jumbled together like a pile of Abby's Pick Up Stix.

"She... me... no... pulled... I..." he tried to explain to his friend, who grabbed Miranda by the arm.

"Don't bother explaining," Harold said with disgust. "I've seen her games so many times that nothing can surprise me anymore."

Right at that point, Adriana tripped, and

though she didn't fall, when she looked up, the whole room was staring at her.

"Adriana!" Miranda exclaimed as Harold finished his sentence with, "Except that." All three of them moved towards her, but before they could speak, she turned quickly and ran back down the hall and down two flights of stairs, stopped to pick up her purse and fur, and then called the first cab she found in the street.

"Take me home," she told the cabbie as she climbed in and slammed the door. "1805 Madison Street." Then she felt her whole body give way, and she settled into a deep sleep.

Lida turned the TV volume all the way down when she heard someone stumble up the walkway, and then a loud knock reverberated through the first floor. Her heart pounded, and she wondered who could be out there at this hour without a key? Muggers? Rapists? She grabbed the phone from the table near the sofa, hit 9-1-1, and put her finger on the DIAL key but waited to press until she saw who was out there. Then she lifted a chair from the kitchen, almost her weight and twice as difficult to get a grip on, and struggled to carry it to the door where she used it to see through the keyhole.

What she saw was worse. Her mother—hair pushed to one side, strap off her shoulder, and makeup soaked in her pores and down her face—stood near the door, sobbing. She was drunk, that much was evident by the way she swayed back and forth in and out of Lida's line of vision, and she kept mumbling something about Lida's father being a son of a bitch.

"Mom," Lida said sharply through the door, and Adriana's head snapped to attention.

"Lida?" Adriana lisped, pushing her ear to the door and giving Lida a close-up view of the huge black circles under her eyes.

"Who else would it be?"

"Oh honey, I'm so glad you're awake. Can you unlock the door, please? I think your father has my keys." Adriana lifted her clutch to the keyhole to demonstrate its emptiness, and Lida rolled her eyes.

"You're drunk."

"I know, I'm sorry. Can you just let me in the house?"

Lida thought of the first time when she had seen her mother drunk, almost six years ago now, when she woke up to the sound of yelling and wandered to the balcony for a front row seat of one of her mother's alcohol-driven brawls. Adriana had been barely able to stand, and though she cursed at Mark, he was the one holding her up by a tight grip on her shoulder.

"No," Lida said forcefully.

"What, honey?"

"I said no. You're not coming in the house like that. What if Abby sees you?"

"Lida Maria, you let me in the house right now or–"

"Or what? You'll put me in time out? I hate to break it to you, but I'd be happy to sit in my room for a month if it means keeping Abby from seeing what a drunk you are."

Silence from the other side of the door. Then Adriana started crying again, only this time it was with small whimpers and dabs at her eyes.

Lida sighed, then opened the door and looked down at her mother. "Not a sound," she warned, putting a finger to her lips. Drunk Adriana mimicked her, finger on lipstick, and then followed her eldest daughter up the stairs to the master bedroom.

Instead of changing, Adriana slipped out of her shoes and then got right into bed in her silky red dress. Lida pulled the covers up, and Adriana's eyes drooped. She reeked of wine, and the drinks had stained her lips red like a zombie in a horror movie.

"I'm going to turn the light off now. Call if you need me," Lida whispered.

Adriana's eyelids struggled open. "Your father's...well... he and Miranda...."

"I know. The late nights at the office? The lipstick on his neck? Seriously, mom, it's not rocket science, you just never pay attention." She didn't add *to anyone but yourself*, but the words hung in the air.

"Oh Lida, I'm sorry."

Lida felt the tears smart on her cheeks, so she quickly turned the light off and shut the door. Before putting herself to bed, she checked on Abby, who was still snoring soundly in the room at the end of the hall. The little girl lay curled in a fetal position, both arms wrapped around a teddy bear that was almost as big as her, and she was surrounded by every toy she had ever asked for, including a thousand dollar plastic castle big enough for both Lida and Abby to sit in and a whole closet of designer princess dresses she would soon outgrow. Lida hoped for Abby's sake that it would be enough.

A BATTLE OF WILLS

Jamison Green called his secretary, Carrie, into the office and sat her down in the leather chair in front of his computer. His face glowed, red with sweat, and he paced a few times in front of his desk before sitting down on the sofa opposite her.

"Are you okay, sir?"

"I need you to type that message," he said, pointing to the little red light glowing above the telephone keypad that indicated a new voicemail. "It's important."

"Yes sir, of course."

Jamison was the General Manager of Rolling Hills Club, a women's club on the outskirts of Philadelphia, and Carrie had worked for him every weekday since graduating from college. He was a likable man, always the first to wish an employee happy birthday or send flowers after surgery, and she had rarely seen him as agitated as he was that morning.

The receiver was damp with his sweat, so Carrie ran her shirt over the plastic and then pressed it to her ear. The woman's voice on the message was clipped and formal, like a set of arrows released at a target in succession, typical of the ladies Carrie had to deal with on a daily basis.

"Hello Mr. Green, this is Mary Martin calling. You and I spoke a few months ago about my mother, Mrs. Daniel Martin, and her... situation. Yet just a week ago, you can imagine my surprise when she informed me that she had visited the Club and had a nice lunch with friends from her garden group. I will be coming in to the office to finalize paperwork on Friday, and I expect to meet with you about the plan moving forward should another attempt occur."

Jamison called women like this a "big fish." Carrie rewound the recording, but it seemed the woman had hung up before giving her contact information. She printed the exact wording and handed the paper to Jamison, then paused by his shoulder until he dismissed her or asked for further assistance.

"Will she be coming in today?" she asked him, and he startled.

"Yes, I think so. Will you come in and take notes when she arrives?"

"Of course, sir." It was not unusual for her boss to ask her to sit in on meetings, but rarely for confidential ones.

At exactly 11:00 A.M., Ms. Martin Jr. arrived in the doorway of Carrie's office. She wore a dark green felt suit fitted to her ample curves, a green vintage fedora from the fifties, and black gloves like stockings all the way up her arms. Her hair fell in an engineered waterfall around her face, making her look more like a dark Doris Day than the modern woman Carrie had been expecting. As she walked closer to Carrie's desk, she could smell mothballs and dust.

"Mary Martin," the woman said as she removed her gloves and tucked them into her Chanel pocketbook. "Here to see Mr. Jamison Green."

"Of course, Ms. Martin," she said, chastising herself for not looking up whether the woman was married so that she could refer to her by proper title, "he is expecting you. Follow me, please."

Carrie was conscious of her plain black suit and dented heels as they walked down the short hallway to Jamison's office. Mary was probably giving her a once-over with raised eyebrows and a wicked smile, maybe even pitying the young secretary for her position. Though she lived in the twenty-first century outside of the Club, inside Carrie felt like just another working-class nobody.

"Ms. Martin," Jamison said, ungluing himself from his sticky leather seat behind the computer and walking over to shake her hand. Mary extended a few fingers as if she was dipping them in nail polish remover, and Jamison clasped the ends and shook them once before letting go.

"Mr. Green, I won't waste much of your time." Translation: you are already wasting my time, and I want this to be over as soon as possible. "As you know, my mother, Mrs. Daniel Martin, has been a member of the Club for over fifty years, as was her mother and her mother's mother before her. Unfortunately, my mother is elderly and no longer mentally well, and as her power of attorney, I have decided that it is no longer financially feasible (nor justified) for her to continue her membership at your fine establishment. I had my secretary fax your accountant the paperwork yesterday, so she should be officially resigned as of March 5 at 5:00 P.M."

"Yes, thank you–"

"Wonderful, I'm glad we understand each other." She opened her purse and pulled out her gloves, then meticulously pulled the black mesh over her thin arms. "Now, if you'll excuse me, I have a Board meeting for the Children's Health Forum to attend and I'm already late." Ms. Martin rose, and this time, she did not extend her hand again. Carrie swung the wooden door open, and before either of them could say another word, Mary Martin was gone.

"Well, that was odd," Carrie said as she perched on the arm of the sofa facing her boss.

"Not for her, it isn't. I've heard things about that woman: multiple divorces, estranged children, and backstabbing friends; the usual, only worse." He sighed, and Carrie could tell it would be an Aspirin at noon kind of day. "Children's Forum... now that's irony."

"I'll go and double check her mother's file with

accounting," Carrie said as she walked towards the door. "Oh, sir, I forgot to mention, I saw your wife's number come up as I was bringing Ms. Martin back. And don't forget to give me the building floor plan for the architect so I can fax it to his assistant, we'll need an agenda for the staff meeting at one, and before I leave for the day, I want to go over your itinerary for your trip to London next week."

Jamison stared at her through his tired, red eyes, and then he pressed his index fingers to his temples. "Thank you, Carrie, I don't know what I'd do without you."

"Let's hope you never have to find out."

"Oh, and Carrie?"

"Yes, sir?"

"Can you bring me an Aspirin and some water?"

Two weeks later, Carrie was filling in for Jared, the receptionist, when she saw the name Mrs. Martin signed on one of the valet chits. She looked up to see an elderly woman in her eighties wearing a bright pink suit and pink cane with purple flowers all the way down, whose hair curled up a few inches like a spurting sink before landing on her bony shoulders.

"Mrs. Daniel Martin?" Carrie asked.

"That's me, all eighty-three years," Mrs. Martin said with a cackle, then stopped laughing and studied Carrie's face. "My lovely daughter has been to see you already, hasn't she?"

"She has, yes, and technically, your club privileges have expired."

"Let me guess, I'm not well, both physically and mentally, and I've been put in a home for my own benefit?"

"Something like that."

"Bunch of hogwash. When your daughter wants your money, and she knows every doctor, lawyer, and nursing home owner in the city, it's not a fair fight."

"No, I imagine it's not. But either way, she canceled your membership."

Mrs. Martin turned at the sound of the door opening and in came Rosemary Anderson, another member and the stepmother of the President of the Rolling Hills Special Events Committee. Carrie knew her well from her stepdaughter's affiliation, as well as the scandal of both Miranda's mother and stepmother holding memberships at the same time. Plus, she was one of only two redheads in the entire club.

"I'm here with this stunning young woman," Mrs. Martin said, hobbling over to Rosemary and enveloping her waist in a hug.

"Betty! I'm so glad to see you," Rosemary said, kissing the older woman on both cheeks. "It will be such a relief to hear your advice on our museum's new exhibits; it's a daunting task."

"Always a pleasure." Mrs. Martin took Rosemary's arm, winked at Carrie, and then followed Rosemary into the dining room.

Carrie discreetly dialed Jamison's extension. "Sir, I just wanted to let you know... not a problem exactly, but Mrs. Daniel Martin came in for lunch with Rosemary Anderson. Rosemary is a member, so there is no issue with her inviting whomever she wants, but I just wanted to let you know... I'll be on the lookout."

True to Carrie's instinct, about twenty minutes later, Ms. Martin pulled up in the back of a Rolls Royce and stomped up the stairs to Carrie's seat at the front desk. She wore a similar suit today, only this one was royal blue with white pearl-colored gloves and matching heels. Though the Club usually smelled a bit musty and old, Ms. Martin's antique clothes overwhelmed even the Club's scent.

"I was told my mother escaped from her nursing home and came here," Ms. Martin said immediately as she glared at Carrie down her pointy nose.

"Mrs. Martin is the guest of Mrs. Anderson."

"I don't care if she's here with the Pope, she is in no state to leave her apartment."

"Ms. Martin, unfortunately–"

"I'll find her myself," Mary said, then huffed away in the opposite direction of the dining room.

Before Carrie could call Jamison for backup, Miranda Anderson walked through the front door like a breeze. "I'm incredibly late," she said to no one in particular, then approached Carrie and struggled with her name despite meeting Carrie at almost every club function and committee meeting for the past five years.

"Carrie," Carrie said after a delay.

"Yes, of course, nice to meet you. I'm meeting my stepmother and Mrs. Daniel Martin for lunch, did they already go in?"

"I believe so. I should probably warn you, Mrs. Martin's daughter is here to try to take her mother back to her home. Mrs. Martin is no longer a member, and Ms. Martin seems to think her mother is in no position–"

"To eat lunch?" Miranda chuckled. "That dinosaur—and I'm speaking of the younger Ms. Martin—gets more cantankerous by the year, and she's only fifty. Just point me to her."

Carrie offered to take Miranda to the table, and as they walked towards the Dining Room, they saw Ms. Martin walking directly in front of them. "Shh,"

Miranda said, putting a finger to her lips. As they got closer to the table, they could hear the snake-like hiss of Ms. Martin's angry voice as she lectured her mother on her unacceptable behavior.

"Your doctor ordered strict bed rest for the entire month, and you are not to leave your apartment, especially when it involves spending my money on lunches you can't afford–"

"Mary?" Miranda asked from behind her.

Ms. Martin stopped her angry rant and turned slowly to face Miranda. "How nice to see you again, Miranda, it's been years."

"Indeed. I'm here to have lunch with these lovely women, and I happened to overhear your quite vicious and inappropriate attack–"

"You don't understand, my mother is under strict house arrest–"

"On what appears to be a quiet, intimate lunch on my club account–"

"I hadn't realized–"

"And furthermore, as you are the only person in this marvelous dining room who is not a member of the club or an invited guest, I would assume that the establishment has the right to forcibly remove you if necessary."

"I think you misunderstand my intentions–"

"Ms. Martin, I understand your intentions perfectly. Now understand mine: Rosemary and I are in the process of renovating an entire wing of a museum, and would like the advice of your experienced mother as we move forward on this immense project. We enjoy her company, and will invite her to dine with us here at the club or elsewhere whenever we see fit. If you interrupt our work a second time, I promise you I will have you removed from the premises with a gaggle of hungry reporters waiting for your exit. Do I make myself clear?"

"Yes, I understand." Ms. Martin shot a final glare at her mother, then turned on her heels and left the dining room as quickly as possible.

Miranda took her seat in the third chair at the table, and Rosemary put her sun-spotted hand over her daughter's.

Carrie grinned and began to walk back to her post at the front door, but before she could get far, Miranda called her back with one of her typical attempts at Carrie's name: "Oh, Ellie?"

"Yes, Mrs. Anderson?"

"Can I get a gin and tonic, please?"

"Well, I'm actually not part of the dining room staff—"

"And some of those cheese straws, the ones they serve at the Fall Ball?"

"As I said, I don't really work in this department, and I'm not sure they still have those—"

"Great, thank you so much."

Miranda turned her back on the girl, leaving the secretary to admire her long, onyx hair with envy. Carrie wrote Miranda's order on a piece of club stationery she had in her pocket and made her way to the back of the dining room to find a serving tray.

"What are you doing back here?" Jamison asked when he found her in the kitchen trying to convince the chef to make a batch of cheese sticks.

Carrie sighed. "I caught a bigger fish."

IN FASHION

When Janet Reynolds's maid handed her a slip of paper with the daily messages in her sloppy half-cursive handwriting, Janet saw the name "Miranda" on the first line and jumped as much as her four-inch heels would allow. The message revealed what Janet already knew: Miranda, Janet's best friend and neighbor, had been chosen to be the Director of the Rolling Hills Club's yearly Fashion Show. Not only that, but she wanted to discuss modeling the spring lines of designers who belonged to the Club when Janet had a spare moment.

Janet's twenty-year-old daughter, Gwen, usually showed little interest in the Club; then again, Janet had practically forced Gwen to become a Younger Member after handpicking the girl's sponsors and bribing her by paying the monthly dues with her second husband's credit card. Janet rushed to the phone extension in her walk-in closet so that Gwen wouldn't overhear her, closed the French doors, and found Miranda's phone number in her Club directory. She knew her daughter would want no part in the fashion show. Gwen often went on tirades about Rolling Hills, especially the cattiness of the older women and the lack of intellectualism present in the younger ones, so Janet figured she would make all of the arrangements and then casually drop the event into a conversation while handing her daughter a nice necklace or new dress. Besides, after the college bills for Gwen's French Studies degree from Brown, her daughter owed her one complaint-free day at the Club.

The phone rang once on the other end, and then Miranda answered in an almost yell, "Janet, my darling! I've been waiting here all afternoon for your call."

"I just got your message," Janet said, "I've been running around all day getting my hair done and donating this terrible antique dish set my mother-in-law gave us for our anniversary. You would die if you saw these plates; whoever invented gray Melmac should be shot."

"If only, but at least they'll find a more appropriate home. Now, about my request–"

"I can't tell you how touched we are that you thought of the Reynolds family! Gwen would be more than happy to model the spring lines."

"My dear, let me stop you right there. I think your maid may have misunderstood my message; I want you to model at the Fashion Show next month!"

"Me? I don't understand."

"The last thing the attendees want to see is a twenty-something anorexic girl in a size 0 dress that would look terrible on a more... realistic woman. We want to show the members that this line is right for everyone, and the only way to do that is to put the clothes on some of our most attractive ladies. Of course, I thought of you right away; you're not a pound over your college weight, and you would look marvelous in some of the sundresses and tight Capri pants we want to show off. It would only take a few hours to get ready, and it would mean so much to me if you'd do it!"

"Of course!" Janet said with more enthusiasm than she felt. "That would be marvelous."

After she hung up, Janet walked out of her closet in a daze. In front of her was the floor-length cast iron peacock mirror her mother had given her on her twentieth birthday, and she walked towards it slowly. Despite the blond hair dye and the fashionable bob, the white Gucci silk-crepe dress and matching D&G sandals, and a pound of concealer, there was no question that her age was showing more and more every day. She could still see the ghost of her former self on days when the light shone just right through the colonial grille, but the rest of the time she saw more she recognized in Gwen than herself. And even worse, her daughter had to waste all of that beauty on ripped jeans and tank tops.

"Mom!" Gwen yelled from outside the bedroom door, wrenching Janet from her trance. "Are you on the phone?"

"No, dear, come on in."

Gwen entered the room in her typical atrocious attire: a green peasant top and blue jeans with green vines on the back pockets. Before Janet could say a word, Gwen launched into a tirade.

"I saw the note on the kitchen counter. Don't you even think of telling Miranda that I'd be *delighted to participate in such an important event.*"

"Gwen—"

"There is no way I'm wearing some ridiculous outfit designed by a misogynist whose whole purpose is to keep women in their place through a combination of sexualization and physical agony."

"Gwen—"

"No, I absolutely won't do it, and there's nothing you can do to convince me."

Sometimes Janet thought that sending her ultra-liberal daughter to college was the worst mistake she had ever made.

"They didn't call for you, Sweetie." She waited for Gwen to cringe at her least favorite nickname, then continued, "They were calling for me. I'm the one who is going to model, along with a few of the other ladies, so that there will be realistic women of all shapes and sizes represented."

Though just minutes before Janet had been

planning ways to get out of the show, the satisfaction of watching her daughter deflate like a pair of collagen lips was worth every minute.

On the day of the Fashion Show, Janet arrived at Rolling Hills a few hours early to have her hair and makeup done. The first floor of the Club was empty, but she could hear laughter coming from the second floor dressing room where the models waited.

The ladies had practiced on the rented catwalk a week before; they walked up and down the stairs in their heels, got measured by the representatives from the stores, and learned a few spins and poses from one of the girls who had been a real model over twenty years ago. Watching the middle-aged women well past their prime strut their stuff on the risers made Janet feel both proud of her friends for their confidence and dismayed at how much had changed since they joined the Club, but she did her best to feign confidence for the sake of the group's morale.

When she entered the dressing room, the comforting smell of perfume and new clothes calmed her nerves. Most of her friends were already dressed, and it was amazing how much a little hair dye, a pair of slimming stockings, and professional makeup could do for a lady. One of the artists led her to a chair and began to wipe her face, while another placed a strand of pearls around her neck.

"Careful with the jewelry, girls!" Miranda teased from the other side of the room. "We wouldn't want you to have to sell your homes to pay for it."

After the makeup artists moved on to another model and a matronly woman in jeans dressed her in a spring suit, Janet sat in the swivel chair to await her cue and stared at her reflection as she had weeks before. This time she saw someone she recognized—her girlish pink cheeks, the sunny blond hair she got from her father, the breasts not yet affected by years of gravity—and she wished she could preserve the reflected image like a glossy magazine cutout. She would never look this good again.

"Janet, you're up!" Miranda hissed from the hall.

Janet scurried out of the chair, around the corner, up the stairs, and then began her confident walk down the aisle. The music was loud, and Miranda was saying something about the designer, but Janet tuned her friend out and relaxed into the rhythm of her step.

Then, out of the corner of her eye, she saw a familiar face at the head table next to the Club President and Activities Chair. It was Gwen, and yet it wasn't; the girl at the table wore a cream-colored suit and delicate hat perched on her head, and her normally nested hair was curled around her face. Her daughter waved, too quickly for anyone else to notice but her mother, and smiled. Janet fought tears as she posed with one leg bent and a hand on her slim hip, triumphant, at the center of it all.

## LIKE MOTHER

"Jerry, what is this?" Miranda Anderson picked up the bright green t-shirt the maid had so perfectly folded and placed on top of her son's laundry basket and waved it in front of his face.

Accompanied by Disturbed's version of "Land of Confusion" jamming in Jerry's ears, it looked like his mother was pumping the shirt in an imitation fist bang. He pulled one of the buds from its cozy nest near his eardrum, sat up from his afternoon slumber, and reached for the shirt with one lazy, catlike paw.

"It's a t-shirt, mom."

"Yes, I can see that. May I ask why you have a t-shirt for French Club when you don't speak French nor have any interest in their culture beyond their delicious chocolate crepes?"

Didn't she have anything better to do with her afternoons? "Because I joined the French Club at Brown during my last semester. I took French in high school, remember?"

"Yes, of course, I do." Miranda perched on his low dresser, crossed the long, tan legs that her white shorts left exposed, and sat back on her hands. "I also remember that you failed, and the football coach had to plead for a D for almost two weeks before Mr. Beecher passed you."

That, plus his mother had shown up in a mini skirt with a check for a thousand dollars in her pocket. School had never been Jerry's strong point; give the young man a football to throw or a rare foreign car to identify and he was golden, but tests panicked him and papers gave him writer's block. He knew his mother had donated an entire building to Brown to get him in, and even that shiny new gym would not have been enough without his football stats.

"Alright, you got me." Jerry lowered his torso back to the soft hug of the bed, flexing his six pack in the process and watching each muscle ripple under his wife beater. He worried about his muscles like they were his children; now that college had ended, and Coach Brady's inspiration shouting matches were miles away, who would keep Jerry on the treadmill or spot him in his father's unused gym? A life of internships and black suits hovered in the horizon, dampening his late summer plans for Europe like a thick smog, and each flabby bicep or deflated quad represented the slow decline from popular jock to Mr. Anderson.

"I joined for a girl. Happy?" He didn't mention that said girl had also recommended half of his iPod playlist, or that coming home for the first half of the summer had more to do with that girl than his family.

Miranda shot him a triumphant grin, and Jerry marveled at the way a simple smile could transform his forty-five-year-old mother into a woman so flawless she could be on the cover of one of the *Playboys* he ordered off the internet. She jumped off the dresser, lay on her stomach on the bed next to him so that he could see halfway down her enhanced cleavage, crossed her legs like a teenage girl at a sleepover, and put her chin in her hands. "Tell me everything!"

Jerry looked up at the ceiling. "There's not much to tell. She's Janet Reynolds's daughter, she went to Brown, and she has a boyfriend."

"Gwen Reynolds? On the shorter side, skinny, always wearing jeans with holes in them? Long brown hair in desperate need of a good cut and a straightener? I saw her recently... I think she came to the Fashion Show at Rolling Hills Club to watch her mother model." Miranda looked off to her right and tapped her pointer finger on her chin, a bad sign.

"Mom, seriously, don't intervene. I know you like to play matchmaker, but Gwen has a boyfriend on the way to fiancé, and I wouldn't want to come between them because I have a crush."

"Of course not, honey, I was just thinking–"

"Well, stop it. Don't make me regret trusting you."

"You didn't, I pried it out of you. You have no

38          Storylandia, Issue 25

poker face, just like your father." Miranda winked at him, then rolled on her back and stretched. "How about a singles match?"

A week later, Jerry and his father drove through their neighborhood on the way back from one of Harold's work happy hours at some bar in the penthouse of a hotel in silence. Harold wanted Jerry to schmooze with his colleagues all summer—talk shop, play the star athlete card, hint at the skills he learned at Brown as a Business major that could apply to an unrelated field if he got his law degree—so that when he hired his unqualified son as an intern, his partners would at least recognize Jerry's face. The whole operation didn't sit well with his father, Jerry could tell by the way Harold coached him on law theories and case studies whenever they climbed in the back of the Rolls-Royce, but Miranda had insisted that Harold use his connections to secure Jerry's future in the firm.

Jerry loosened his red tie and ruffled his hair out of the gelled coif he'd spent all afternoon perfecting. The young man couldn't get the image of the scantily clad women in tight leather skirts out of his mind: their swish-swish walks as they handed out glasses of expensive Scotch to overweight suits barely balancing on bar stools, their soft touches on his shoulder as they passed him with a tray, their gumption as first one and then another of the girls approached him on a walk to the restroom and slipped her number in his back pocket with a squeeze. By 7:00, he had collected seven numbers on seven receipt corners tucked in his suit pocket which he planned to pursue when not in the company of the men who would decide his future.

"There's an awful lot of cars on our block," Harold said as he sat forward and peered out through the window.

"What?" Jerry readjusted his position on the seat, pushed the imaginary waitress from his thoughts, and focused on the view. "You're right. Someone must be having a party."

Benjamin, their driver, slammed on the brakes, causing both men to buck forwards and Harold to bang his head on the glass.

"What the hell?" his father asked angrily, rubbing his forehead.

"Sorry sir, it's just... there's a girl walking in the middle of your driveway."

Both men got out, and Jerry recognized the back of the woman standing in front of the car immediately. Maybe she did need a haircut, but what she lacked in style she made up for in smarts and enthusiasm. Plus, under the holes in her jeans and t-shirts with "Save the Trees" plastered across her chest, she had a body that almost made Jerry fail English Lit.

"Gwen?"

"Hi, Jerry!"

"What are you doing here?"

Gwen blushed. "It was supposed to be a surprise, but I'm late."

"For what?" Harold asked, looking up at the lighted house. Suddenly he could hear the bass drum and laughter emanating out of the thirty front windows.

"Your graduation party!"

Jerry looked at his father, his father looked at Benjamin, Benjamin shrugged his shoulders, and then they both looked at Jerry.

"Don't look at me," he said, "I had nothing to do with this."

"Of course not, it was supposed to be a

surprise!" Gwen wrapped him in a hug, handed him a card, and put her arm through his. "Your mother felt terrible that she didn't plan something for you when you got back, but with the Fashion Show and other club commitments, it just slipped her mind!"

Jerry could practically see the strings moving Gwen's mouth and hands. His mother must have called her and spoon-fed her that garbage for however long it took to convince her to break her Friday plans and come to Jerry's "graduation party." One person had not been so well informed: Harold's lips pursed in a tight line as Gwen spoke, and his head shook slightly from tensing the muscles in his neck. As a lawyer, Jerry's father rarely got angry; he usually tried logic first, and if that failed (as it often did with Miranda), he either hid in his den or went back to the office. But there had been a few times when Harold had gotten angry in front of Jerry, so angry his hands shook and his voice went so loud the neighbors could hear it through the five-room cushion, and these displays were always directed at his mother. As they stood in the driveway, Harold's face turned as red as his hair, and he took a few deep breaths before Jerry patted him on the shoulder and they all walked into the house together.

When a strange young woman in a pink dress ushered them into their own home, at least fifty people crammed into the hall, stairway, and second floor landing greeted them with an enthusiastic "Surprise!" Jerry surveyed the faces packed like a *Where's Waldo* page, but though he recognized high school friends, a few graduates from Brown, women from his mother's city club, and neighbors from down the street, Miranda was nowhere to be seen. Her fingerprints were everywhere—the classic rented martini glasses, pink punch, appetizers on silver trays carried by banquet staff. The party pulsed with her magnetic energy.

"I'm going to the den," Harold said to Jerry before veering off to the left.

"I want to say hi to your mom," Gwen yelled in Jerry's ear as they fought through the throng of well-wishers.

"My best guess is upstairs in her dressing room curling her hair for the third time. I have to change anyway; I'll take you up."

The crowd dispersed through the house, some to the back patio where Jerry knew they would find a barbecue and others to the kitchen where a rented chef was probably spooning out French delicacies. Crepes, if he had to guess.

"Mom?" Jerry asked through her bedroom door, but only the faint rustle of fabrics answered.

"I think it's safe." Jerry knocked, then swung the door wide open before he realized what was happening on the other side. His mother, wrapped in a tight gold dress that revealed her tan shoulders, had a man pressed up against the wall across the room; a man so young that he wore a college t-shirt and jeans ripped at the knees, combined with hideous brown flip flops that stuck out from behind Miranda's gold heels. Both of their martini glasses sat on the dresser like sentries, empty except the last mouthful of pink liquid, and Jerry guessed his mother had been drinking since the early afternoon.

"Oh, I'm sorry," Gwen said to no one in particular, and Jerry started to close the door. "Wait," she said suddenly, her expression changing. She pushed the door open and stepped into the room, and that's when Jerry realized what he should have guessed as soon as he saw Gwen in his driveway: the man pressed against the wall was Finn, Gwen's boyfriend, who was too busy trying to kiss Miranda to notice the very angry young woman walking towards him.

"Finn?"

Finn stuck his head around Miranda's shoulder. His eyes were bleary and red, and when he spoke, he had a slight lisp. "Gwen? What are you doing here?"

"What are you talking about? I invited you!"

"But Miranda said..."

"Gwen dear, thank you so much for coming!" Jerry's mother interrupted, stepping away from Finn. "Do you know this young man?"

Jerry saw Gwen's hesitation as she tried to read Miranda's face, and for once he hoped someone would see through one of his mother's schemes. But Gwen turned away and began to cry, and when Finn tried to comfort her, she pushed his hand away.

"I don't want to talk to any of you," she said, moving to the door. "Especially you, Finn, we're over. Jerry, I'm so sorry about all of this." Then she disappeared, quickly followed by a contrite, drunk Finn, leaving only Miranda and Jerry in the room.

"Well, that was exciting," Miranda said as she sat down in front of her mirror.

Jerry wanted to throw something, maybe her tray of expensive perfumes, but instead he clenched his hands to his sides. There were guests downstairs, and he didn't want to explain the situation to over fifty outsiders plus his father. "I doubt it since it all went exactly to plan."

"Darling, I don't know what you're referring to." Miranda dabbed her forehead with her powder brush, leaving a little cloud of dust behind. "That boy was obviously not good enough for our Gwen, and now she knows it."

"She's not *our* Gwen; she's not even my Gwen. She's just a girl who got caught in your web, and from now on, I want you to leave her alone."

Miranda shrugged. "My work is done." She picked up her mascara brush and began to stroke her long, black lashes, and Jerry could see the triumph in her cold, brown eyes. "You would have done the same thing; we both always get what we want."

Poor Gwen. He thought of the tears flooding her pretty eyes, still wide from the shock, and shook his head. "You're right, I used to think I was exactly like you. But what I want is for Gwen to have the kind of guy she deserves, and that isn't me." Miranda's eyes fluttered upwards towards her son. Jerry walked to the door, and from there he said looked back at his mother one last time. "Someday, when everyone you love and care about is gone because you 'knew' what you wanted, you're going to realize the difference."

NO DIVING

Harold sat in his home office the Saturday morning after his son's college graduation party, the only one awake in a house full of empty rooms, struggling to concentrate on a difficult case. The housekeeper who cooked their meals and cleaned their rooms would not arrive for another two hours; Harold had found a few biscuits in the pantry and a package of instant coffee to hold him over, which he munched and sipped as he read and reread the papers splayed out on his executive oak desk.

Suddenly, his phone vibrated with a persistent *brrrr brrrr brrrr*. His son slept soundly in the guest bedroom, and his wife had passed out drunk just three hours earlier. Harold cleared his throat, picked up his Blackberry, and answered quietly, "Hello, this is Harold Anderson."

"Harold?" a feminine whisper snuck through the phone, and though Harold couldn't quite place the voice, he knew it. Hopefully, not one of his previous clients, or worse, one of their lovers; he had changed his number five times in nine months because of scorned prostitutes and young social climbers in search of fame and a few extra bucks.

"I'm sorry, who is this?" As he spoke, he jotted the number on a notepad with his name on top, just in case an investigation would be necessary.

"Has it been that long?"

Wait. The voice grew, not in volume but in weight, and the name came to him as an image of a pale white leg wrapped in a cotton sheet flashed in front of his eyes. "Bree? How did you get this number?"

Harold met Bree at his five-year college reunion; two dateless, married lawyers placed next to each other at a prominent table near the stage. Miranda stayed home with Jerry that year, since the nanny was out with the flu and the boy only two; though the couple had struggled in the past few years, Harold missed her social graces and electric energy as he took bites of overcooked chicken and salad drenched in oil and vinegar.

"I hate these things," Bree said, leaning closer to Harold so that her voice carried over the 80s throwbacks that men his age were supposed to enjoy. Under the scent of her gin and tonic, she smelled like men's deodorant, a Speed Stick if he had to guess, the way Miranda used to when she slept in his dorm and borrowed his essentials.

"Me too," he said, moving closer. "I don't even know why I bother."

"Oh come on, you're a lawyer. You're here so you can network with old men you don't like, get business cards, and go home and put those cards in your Rolodex for future needs."

"And women."

"What?"

"You forgot women we don't like. Law is an equal opportunity networking hub now. And what is this 'you' business?"

Bree laughed. "I gave up law when I had my first child, so now I'm even worse than a lawyer; I'm a lawyer's wife. The cards change hands, and then I give them to my husband."

"I understand." Harold pushed his plate aside, hoping for cake. "My wife climbs the social ladder like a child on a playground, and I'm usually the one at the bottom waiting for a hand up."

"She sounds like quite a woman." Bree sipped her drink, still eyeing him over the rim.

"She is."

He thought of their separate bedrooms, Miranda too tired from childcare to tolerate his hopeful caresses let alone reciprocate them, and the sound of the door as it shut slowly each night. Even before Jerry entered the world—a perfect doll quickly accessorized in a blue Ralph Lauren onesie and hat; the childlike face of Miranda staring up at his scrawny, red-haired father with tears in his eyes—a strangeness had existed between them, like the silence in his firm when even the interns had gone home to contemplate suicide. Harold worked all day and night, practically blind by the time he crawled into his empty king sized bed, and Miranda clawed through the tea parties and galas like a soldier through jungle terrain. Too busy to touch, too busy to pause for one minute and remember why they worked day after day to secure a position they would never enjoy.

"Want to get out of here?" Bree asked suddenly as a song wound down to the beat of another beginning. "I miss the Boston nightlife."

"Well..." The baby in blue, the baby in blue, the baby in blue. "Sure, I'd love that."

Bree touched his arm, and he could feel the warmth of her fingertips through his suit jacket. His insides stirred, yearned, and though he knew he shouldn't, he followed her to the coat check.

"Harold?" Bree asked in his ear, and he snapped to attention. "I said I'm coming to the Philly area, and I'd love to see you."

Harold massaged his forehead. "You know I can't do that. I'm married."

"You were married the first time, and that didn't stop you." Again, the toga leg, the hairless angle of her knee.

"I know, but it's been years. Things are different now."

"Not from what I hear. Miranda didn't even bother to cheat with a stranger; she took your best friend to a room in your country club and had her way with him."

Her words cut him, even though the two had only kissed before he discovered them tucked away during the Fall Ball. Bree had transformed into someone bitter, someone spiteful, though who she wanted revenge on remained a mystery.

"Nothing happened, Bree, it was the alcohol talking. Just like what happened to us."

"I want to see you, Harold."

A divorce, most likely, or a death. Though the clock said 8:30 A.M., her voice floated in an alcohol-induced haze. "I don't care what I have to do." He heard the sound of shuffling paper, and then a triumphant "Ah! It's incredible how easy it is to get the contact information of a total stranger."

"You wouldn't dare call her."

"Oh, Harold." The sound of ice against glass, like a wind chime. "You don't know me."

They found a diner, something made of chrome and blue plastic. They drank a whole bottle of Cab from cracked glasses, and their lips soon turned red with the cheap wine. They ordered blueberry pancakes and strawberry cheese crepes that had to be sent back with instructions on the essential quality of cheese filling.

"Who makes cheese crepes without cheese?" Harold asked to no one in particular, and Bree giggled.

"Look at what they did to my pancakes," she said, holding up a limp blueberry pancake with all of the blueberries on one side and twirling it on her fork like a spit.

After they ate their fill and left the rest as a fruity mess on the table, Harold followed Bree to her hotel.

"Let's swim," she said, taking his hand and leading him towards the smell of chlorine.

"It's 1:00 A.M.; the guard is probably gone, and besides, I don't have a suit."

"You don't need one," she said, stripping off her suit jacket as she walked down the hall. She pulled the bobby pins from her bun, releasing a mess of brown curls. When they snuck into the abandoned pool, she threw off her heels, pants, stockings, and thin cotton blouse. Standing in the blue light from the water, she looked like a nymph pulled to land by a greedy sailor. Her body was round under the jacket where Miranda's was taught, but something about the softness of her curves ushered him to seek solace there.

As Bree walked down the cement stairs to the water, Harold undressed in the more forgiving backlight. His skin hadn't seen sun in years, and he had the body of a scholar. Once his clothes were off, he stood at the edge of his pool in just his underwear looking down at Bree like he would watch over a swimming child. His mind faded in and out of comprehension, the alcohol mixing his thoughts like a thin broth, and the lights twinkled and dimmed like the stars through the glass ceiling.

"Coming?" she asked. "It's wonderful."

"My wife doesn't love me anymore," he said as he looked over the water at the sign that said NO DIVING in big, red letters.

She stopped swimming and walked close to where he stood. "No one stays in love," Bree said without her smile, as though it had washed off in the water.

"Then go ahead, if you want to. Call her."

The clinking stopped. "What?"

"I said call her. If you dare."

"What's that supposed to mean? You think I won't?"

Harold spun around so that his chair faced the wall, and he imagined the angry round face staring him down from the plaster. "The opposite, in fact. I know you will. I've been a lawyer for over twenty years, and in that time I have defended over thirty businessmen whose affairs were plastered all over the papers. When I got back from Boston, I told Miranda everything. And I have paid for it dearly ever since."

Silence on the other end, and then Miranda poked her head through the office door. "Harold, Sophia made breakfast. Don't let it get cold."

"Coming." He addressed the woman on the other end, "Thank you for your time, and I'm sorry I'm not free to take the case." Then he hung up, laid the phone on the desk, and walked towards his wife. He put a hand on her back; though she didn't touch him, she didn't pull away.

THE WHITE STORM

If Miranda Anderson had looked up as she exited the Paws Veterinary Hospital with a heavy crate in hand, she might have noticed a strange formation of altostratus clouds as she took her first step towards her pink Porsche. If she had not been distracted as she drove through Philadelphia by her cat, Rufus, who meowed from the passenger seat, the descent of those same mass of particles into dark nimbus clouds might have forced her to drive home instead of stopping at an expensive cat food store for Rufus's new diet. But as the first snowflake fell against her windshield like a kiss, Miranda Anderson was still an hour from home, driving with a Diet Coke in one hand and the "What You Should Know about Feline Diabetes" spreadsheet in the other.

"Damn," she said, rolling down her window and looking up at the billions of flakes falling like sugar on the Earl Grey cityscape. In the minute during which she stopped to look, half an inch had already accumulated on her windshield. Harold had mentioned something about the bad weather during breakfast that she had subsequently ignored, stating that Rufus's health was at stake. Miranda turned to the beady eyes watching through the air holes, glared at Rufus, and grumbled, "You're lucky I love you." Then she made an illegal U-turn and sped through the snowy streets to Rolling Hills Club to see if they had a room.

When the storm hit, the only two employees on duty were Jared, the doorman and substitute desk clerk, and Adelita, the housekeeper. All of the other staff had either called out or gone home when the news of the blizzard spread through the house, but money was money, and those two needed it. Several inches of wet white soon covered the flowerbeds and walkways, and though no guests were expected, Jared went out in a wool coat and winter boots to shovel the paths to and from the driveway.

Mid-shovel, he heard the crunch of tires on the blacktop and then the squeal of breaks. When he turned, he saw the signature Barbie-pink car he had come to dread over his twenty years at the club pulling closer and closer to his spot in the middle of the driveway, and though he didn't believe God cared about such inconsequential matters, he prayed very hard that Mrs. Anderson had not come to spend the night.

"Oh Jared, I'm so glad to see you," Miranda gushed as she pulled herself out of the low leather seat. She wore a white pea coat, tight white jeans, and tall white pumps at least three inches high. Only rich people wear white, Adelita explained to him once as she carried dry cleaning to the sixth floor, because someone else cleans it. Miranda waited by the passenger door, but Jared didn't move to help her with her bags.

"Great, I'll just get these," she mumbled, tugging on a huge animal crate in the front seat of her car. The crate stuck tight, so she placed a heel carefully on the ledge of the car, grabbed the crate from both sides, and pulled with all of her might.

"Lord, give me strength," Jared said as he looked up at the swirling sky. Then he walked to the car to give one of his least favorite patrons a hand. "Whatcha got in here anyway, a horse?" Jared asked, heaving on one side while Miranda yanked on the other.

"A cat, actually."

"Lord Jesus! What you been feeding him, children?"

Miranda pouted. "He's just a little overweight, but we're going to work on that." She put her face up against the air holes. "Aren't we, honey? Yes, we are! We're going to get you so slim no one will even recognize you."

With a final tug, the crate flew towards them, throwing Miranda butt-first into the snow and leaving Jared holding a thirty-five-pound cat. Even crouching with the crate on his thigh, Harold could barely maintain his gloved grasp.

They entered the Great Hall, Miranda with her excessively large purse in tow and Jared with the excessively large crate ready to fall at any minute. Jared set the crate down in front of the reception desk, removed his gloves, and walked around to the computer to complete his official check-in procedures. Meanwhile, Miranda opened the door and began to tempt the creature out of its cave; no luck, so she tilted the whole cage forward and sent the cat sliding down from the bottom of the crate to the floor of the club.

The cat was a monster that dwarfed the Tory Burch tote on the floor next to him, and that swallowed the rose-patterned carpet under his blubber. A monster that inspired fear in the poor receptionist behind the low wall of the front desk, who happened to hate cats since one had scratched him as a child. Rufus had a long, shaggy white coat that matched his mistress's attire, his eyes were round beads of onyx, and his claws flexed and relaxed with every purring breath he took.

The glutinous beast eyed Jared longingly with his predatory gaze, stirred as he saw his prey, focused as Jared retrieved a pen, and perked up as one of Jared's feet touched his paw. Then he strained as his weight battled his desire, and strained and strained, but his muscles had long ago deflated under the weight of his fat. Though the cat tried to fight gravity, his paws refused to lift him and his claws fought to grasp the carpet, a carpet which Adelita cared for every morning and which the cat shredded within minutes.

Right at that moment, the housekeeper happened to pass the front desk on her way to clean the Terrace Bar. At first, she didn't notice the newcomers, and Miranda and Jared watched as Adelita pulled her cleaning cart past the elevator, careful not to overturn the spray bottles and towers of white towels set on top. Just then, the cat howled a deadly meow that sent chills through Jared's heart, and Adelita froze, turned slowly towards the front door, and then uttered just three words: "Ay dios mio."

"Tenemos un invitado," Jared said in his best attempt at Spanish, struggling with the word guest. "¿Que te parece?"

He asked her what she thought, but deep down

they both knew that the GM, Jamison, would fry them for breakfast if he found out they had turned away a guest in the middle of a blizzard. Jared also knew that if the guest in question happened to crash in a snowstorm on her way home, Jamison would never know they rejected her. *Stop that, you're gonna get yourself in more trouble than that lady's worth.*

Adelita considered the pair in front of the desk, then threw her hands up in defeat. As the cart continued to roll down the hall, Jared gave Miranda a serious talk, "Listen, I'm okay with you staying, but know a few things: there's no cook, which means there's no in-house meals. We're the only staff, and we won't be on duty 24/7. Jamison permitted us to use the rooms, so we'll be guests, just like you." Well, close enough.

Miranda looked out of the front windows at the storm that was enveloping the city like a mother's hug. "Yes, I understand." Then she signed the bill for $350 a night, took the skeleton key that opened room 404 (Jared made sure to place her on a different floor than the staff), and dragged her bags to the elevator as Jared feigned occupation with the rest of her paperwork.

Desperation made members gentle, like lions on leashes, but Jared knew better. Eventually, her claws would emerge like Rufus's, and she wouldn't be too fat to kill her prey. *Ay dios mio* was right.

After her run-in with Miranda, Adelita fled to the housekeeping office to finish the laundry and press fresh sheets in case Miranda extended her stay. Like the other employees, Adelita had her share of grievances against Mrs. Anderson, most recently the time she met the housekeeper in the Great Hall.

Miranda had sat with a guest, a young woman about her son's age, and the newcomer kept staring at Adelita as she dusted the lamps and wiped the martini glass stains off of the tables.

"What's wrong, Gwen?" Miranda had asked, looking around for the source of the woman's discomfort.

"It just feels strange, having people clean up your mess every time you move. It makes me feel guilty."

"What people? Oh, you mean the housekeepers? Just pretend they're invisible; that's what they want."

Adelita's thoughts mirrored the steam that rose from the sheets in front of her like a hot bath. Maybe she was invisible; less than a year before that, Adelita had walked in on Miranda and a man who was not her husband kissing in one of the guest bedrooms during one of the balls. Mrs. Anderson had not noticed the creak of the door or the whisper of Adelita's black sneakers on the carpet.

Adelita's husband had died more than five years before the incident, and she remembered how much the two sloppy drunks lying on the bed made her want to scream profanities in any language she knew. To be lucky enough to have a rich, successful husband waiting downstairs to dance with you, and to throw it all away on some selfish game... it was enough to make her sick.

A knock came at the door. "It's me," Jared said, "are you decent?"

"For the last time," Adelita grumbled as she rose from her chair, "we change in the locker room."

As she opened the door, Jared leaned in and raised his eyebrows at her. "A man can only hope, mi amor."

"Your Spanish is terrible."

"It's all for you, baby."

"Can I help you with something?"

"I have a surprise for you."

Jared had begun working at the club five years after Adelita, and she remembered the way he swaggered in with a black top hat over his curly black hair and asked for a job as doorman even though they had not advertised the position. "You need me," he told an appalled Jamison, and he had been right; just a week later, their doorman had left them for the Gerard Club, and Jared returned in a suit and shiny black shoes for his first day on the job. He lived in the city with his three daughters, sans a wife who passed away when the children were just babies, and he spent more hours at the club than the house he struggled to pay for. In his free time, he hunted Adelita with a teenager's stamina. Every Valentine's Day, for five years, he had brought her a dozen roses, and every Christmas a necklace featuring a different rare stone.

"I brought you this," he said, dangling something silver and shiny in front of her face.

"I told you, no more jewelry," she said, but when she grasped the metal in her hand and looked down, she realized the object was a key.

"You get the suite, baby. You've earned it."

"But Mrs. Anderson...?"

"I told her the room was out of service. You're more of a lady than she'll ever be, and now you get to live it—well, at least until the snow stops. Enjoy it."

Adelita grabbed his arm and squeezed. "Thank you, Jared."

"No problem."

He turned to go, but a thought occurred to her and she called down the stairs, "You don't have a key to the bedroom, do you?"

"Don't worry," he called back, "I don't need one. Someday you're going to just let me in."

The suite was on the fifth floor, and during her lunch break, Adelita wandered to room 506 with a few belongings from her locker. The fifth floor fell under the other housekeepers' responsibility, so the suite gleamed with the shine of someone else's hard labor. The suite was a large, circular room twice as big as the others, with a canopy bed and plush green sofa near the floor-length windows that looked out onto the city. The green walls reminded her of light reflected on leaves, and she traced their white border with a lazy finger as she circled her temporary home. An old wooden desk sat on the far side of the room, its paper notepads perfectly stacked and a Rolling Hills Club pen angled on top, as if the founder of the club had just laid her work down and never returned.

An old fashioned phone sat on the dresser nearby, and Adelita picked it up and dialed her daughter's cell phone. The call went to voicemail, service suspended from the storm, and Adelita thanked God she could rely on her sister to watch the precocious fourteen-year-old. "Hola mi hija," she said, her voice strange as it echoed around the circular ceiling. "You'll never guess where I'm sitting right now."

For two days, the storm barraged the city with snow, hail, and sleet. The height of the snow rose against the club's first-floor windows like a tide, and Miranda, Jared, and Adelita watched in growing anticipation as the white jaws enveloped the building.

Miranda holed up in her room attempting to use her cell phone and drinking half the bar, Jared read newspaper after newspaper at the front desk, and Adelita cleaned with a determined rage.

The club had never looked so spotless, but with only three people drinking, eating canned soup, and sleeping, even Adelita ran out of chores by the third day. And so it was that all three guests ended up in the Terrace Bar at dinner time the next night, two on one side of the room and the third on the other, waiting for someone to speak.

Eventually, Miranda got up and searched through the liquor closet for a bottle of red wine. She had realized that the snow would last another few days, and she needed to talk to someone before she went mad. "How about this one?" she said when she emerged holding a hundred dollar bottle, and Adelita and Jared exchanged a look that she couldn't read.

"It's on me, just add it to my tab. If my husband wants to leave me holed up in this club for a week, so be it," she muttered more to herself than them. "I'll rack up a bill so high he won't see straight for days." Then she found a wine opener, popped the cork, and poured a generous glass for each of the employees.

Despite sharing the wine, Miranda was an outcast while the other two discussed plans for escape or complained about the situation in Spanish. As the night that surrounded them drew closer, pulling whoever sat in the room into a huddle, and as the light that protected them grew dim, causing whoever saw it a moment of comfort, Miranda poured more wine into whichever clean classes were available and onto whatever surface got in her way, a way that would lead through the eight feet of snow, a trail that would push through the choked streets, a guide that would direct her to her husband and son. A husband and son who she hoped had noticed her absence as she drowned in the half-empty cup, staining her white Ralph Lauren pants red.

She approached the pair on the other side of the room, her drunken steps as crooked as a bird's tracks. "I can't wear this outfit another day," she stated.

Adelita stared at her, then said in harsh, unbroken English, "What exactly do you want us to do about it?"

"You speak English? But I thought–"

"You didn't think anything, *princesa*, don't flatter yourself."

Jared grabbed Adelita's shoulder and whispered that she needed to calm down, but she continued to glare at Miranda with eyes like the tips of arrows trained on hers. "I don't care," she said to Jared without looking away, "they can fire me. I'm done."

"I must have missed something..."

"I heard you that day with Gwen when you said all the workers here wanted to be invisible. Well, guess what, we may have to clean up your dirty glasses and the sheets you stain with another man, but you're the one who's really invisible." Adelita rose, bringing her face within inches of Miranda's, and the scents of laundry detergent and lilac air fresheners overwhelmed the Merlot's sweet residue. "You're a surface, a mirror, and underneath there's nothing but empty air."

Not exactly, Miranda thought as Adelita left the room and Jared followed her. Even a surface has a shadow.

The next morning, Adelita heard a persistent knock on the housekeeping door. "Jared, if this is about apologizing, I'm telling you for the millionth time that I'm not..." She stopped when she saw a white heel enter first, followed by Miranda Anderson.

Miranda must have carried enough makeup in her purse to cover her face like a Macy's model because even in the middle of a snowstorm with one outfit, her eyeshadow changed colors every morning.

"Hi," Miranda said, approaching the housekeeper slowly as she would a wild dog.

"Hi."

The two women looked at each other for a few minutes, and then Adelita broke the silence, "How can I help you?"

"I thought..." Miranda started to say, then trailed off as she circled the housekeeping headquarters. She touched the large machine the women used to iron the sheets, grazed her fingertips along the edge of the dryers, and ended at the shelf where the rows of cook and housekeeper uniforms waited in piles of five. Then she delicately lifted one of the black housekeeper's uniforms from the top of a stack, unfolded it, and held it to her body. "Perhaps I can borrow one of these?"

"You're kidding."

"I wish I was. I need a second set of clothes while these go in the wash, and unless I concoct a toga from one of the linens, this is my only option."

"Fine, take it. But not that one, that's an extra-large."

Miranda looked down at the dress in front of her, at least four times the width of her waist, and giggled. Adelita tried to hold her laughter back, but she couldn't help smiling at the sight of Miranda Anderson behind a uniform she could have used as a tent.

Miranda took one of the smaller uniforms and walked towards the door. There she paused, turned, and said, "I'm not going to tell anyone what you said last night."

"Sure," Adelita said, turning back to her work.

"No really, I'm not. You were right."

"You say that now, but the minute you leave this club, you'll go back to being Miranda Anderson, millionaire's wife and most dreaded member."

"How can I convince you?"

"You can't."

"Listen, we may be trapped in here for weeks, and I don't want to spend every night under suspicion. So I have a deal for you; I'll keep what you said a secret, and you can take a picture of me in this ridiculous uniform. If I break my word, you can spread it around. Deal?"

Adelita whipped out her cell phone, nothing more than a camera after the storm killed the power lines. "Okay, deal."

As it turned out, Miranda was not entirely useless after all. Once she donned the black dress with silver buttons, securing the extra fabric in a safety pin behind her back, and a pair of extra shoes from Adelita's locker, she transformed into a woman who found her way to the kitchen in the basement, got the gas stoves working, and within hours began producing meals that rivaled those served to the membership on Easter or Christmas. "We didn't always have servants," Miranda hinted, but she didn't say more. Neither of the employees could figure out when she had learned to cook between her father's house, where Adelita's great-uncle worked in Mr. Anderson's kitchen, and her own home, where Adelita's neighbor labored ten hours a day. After they took the first bite of sautéed mushrooms over penne instead of cans of soup or the food bars Jared had bought before the worst of the storm closed all of the nearby stores, they stopped caring.

Seven days into their seclusion, Miranda, Jared, and Adelita were on their way to the dining room with hot plates of mushroom ravioli when Miranda stopped short and dropped her plate.

"What's wrong?" Adelita asked from behind her, unable to see past Miranda to the man standing in the doorway and more focused on the soy sauce now permeating her clean carpet than the rescue about to unfold.

"Harold?" Miranda asked, taking a tentative step towards him. He looked great in his winter garb, a long black coat and black cap from their trip to England years before that revealed a rim of red hair around his face, and though she wanted to touch him, she was wary after all of the fights they had before the day she left with Rufus. Would he ever forgive her for what she had done? But when she walked over to her husband and started to speak, he grabbed her in a bear hug and swung her around, ignoring the curious stares of the two hungry staff behind them.

"How did you find me?" she asked in wonder.

"The storm's been over for a day! I followed the trail of my credit card, which led here."

"A day?" She looked out of the window and realized that he was right; none of them had noticed that the snow had slowed to a dusting and then stopped, allowing plows into the city to pave the way home.

"It's good to see you, Miranda. But may I ask... what the hell are you wearing?"

"Oh, this? It's a long story."

Adelita and Jared started to walk to the dining room, already fading into the background, but Miranda called them back.

"Harold, I want you to meet two very good

friends of mine. If it weren't for them, I would never have survived the storm. Meet Adelita and Jared, the Rolling Hills Club's two finest employees. Adelita and Jared, meet Harold, my husband."

"Friends?" Harold said softly in her ear. "Who are you and what have you done with my wife?"

"What do I always tell you?" Miranda said, walking towards the elevator to pack her belongings, shove Rufus into his crate, and change into her white pants. "Desperation." Then she looked at the man and woman holding plates of her food, two new friends who had changed her forever and who one day soon would join her in marriage's day-to-day struggle after spending the first few days of their relationship trapped in the city club where they worked. "And thank goodness for it."

Kelly Ann Jacobson is the author or editor of many published books, including novels such as Cairo in White, the poetry collection I Have Conversations with You in My Dreams, and anthologies such as Dear Robot: An Anthology of Epistolary Science Fiction. She also writes young adult fantasy novels under her pen name, Annabelle Jay. Kelly received her MA in Fiction at Johns Hopkins University and is now working toward her PhD in Fiction at Florida State University. Her work—including short stories published in such places as Northern Virginia Review and Iron Horse Literary Review—can be found at www.kellyannjacobson.com or www.annabellejay.com

Thank you to the Wapshott Press sponsors, supporters, and Friends of the Wapshott Press.

Muna Deriane

Kathleen Warner

Rachel Livingston

James and Rebecca White

Jennifer Bentson

Debbie Jones

Steven Acker

Ann Siemens

Suzanne Siegel

Aubrey Hicks

Carol Colin

Ted Waltz

Kathleen Bonagofsky

Cynthia Henderson

Nancy Lilly

Jeff Morawetz

Patricia Nerad

Amanda Nerad

Elaine Padilla

Laurel Sutton

Deana Swart

The Wapshott Press is a 501(c)(3) not-for-profit enterprise publishing work by emerging and established authors and artists. We publish books that should be published. We are very grateful to the people who believe in our plans and goals, as well as our hopes and dreams. Our new website is at www.WapshottPress.org

www.ingramcontent.com/pod-product-compliance
Lightning Source LLC
Chambersburg PA
CBHW071204130626
46555CB00004B/1578